A NOTE TO PARENTS

When your children are ready to "step into reading," giving them the right books is as crucial as giving them the right food to eat. **Step into Reading Books** present exciting stories and information reinforced with lively, colorful illustrations that make learning to read fun, satisfying, and worthwhile. They are priced so that acquiring an entire library of them is affordable. And they are beginning readers with a difference—they're written on five levels.

Early Step into Reading Books are designed for brand-new readers, with large type and only one or two lines of very simple text per page. **Step 1 Books** feature the same easy-to-read type as the Early Step into Reading Books, but with more words per page. **Step 2 Books** are both longer and slightly more difficult, while **Step 3 Books** introduce readers to paragraphs and fully developed plot lines. **Step 4 Books** offer exciting nonfiction for the increasingly independent reader.

The grade levels assigned to the five steps—preschool through kindergarten for the Early Books, preschool through grade 1 for Step 1, grades 1 through 3 for Step 2, grades 2 through 3 for Step 3, and grades 2 through 4 for Step 4—are intended only as guides. Some children move through all five steps very rapidly; others climb the steps over a period of several years. Either way, these books will help your child "step into reading" in style!

Step into Reading™

The Emperor's Birthday Suit

By Cindy Wheeler

Illustrated by
R.W. Alley

A Step 2 Book

Random House 🏠 New York

Once there lived an Emperor
who loved new clothes.
He had so many suits
that he never wore
the same one twice!

At the palace

the royal helpers were always

weaving more cloth…

sewing more suits…

building more closets…

and oohing and aahing

over the Emperor's new clothes!

And yet, the Emperor

was never happy.

One morning two strangers
were passing by the palace.
They heard the Emperor
shouting at his helpers.

"I have nothing to
wear for my birthday!
I want a suit
that is like no other.
I want a suit that is
<u>extra special!</u>"

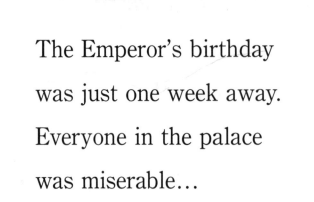

The Emperor's birthday
was just one week away.
Everyone in the palace
was miserable…

But outside the palace
the strangers were laughing.
They had thought of a clever idea.
It would make them rich!

The strangers asked
to speak to the Emperor.

"I am Mr. Bobbin," said one.

"I am Mr. Thread," said the other.

"So?" said the unhappy Emperor.

"We are tailors," said the strangers.

"We are here to make you a new suit.

A suit that is like no other!

A suit that is extra special!"

"Really!" said the Emperor.

"How is it extra special?"

"We spin a very fine thread
from gold and silver coins,"
said Mr. Bobbin.

"And into each piece of cloth
we weave a little magic!"
said Mr. Thread.

"What kind of magic?"

asked the Emperor.

"Wise people can see the cloth,

but fools cannot!" said Mr. Thread.

A suit that fools couldn't see!

That would indeed be

a suit like no other!

The Emperor told the tailors

to begin at once.

The royal helpers took the tailors

to the royal sewing room.

Then they brought in

three bags of gold coins

and three bags of silver coins.

The tailors said

they needed these coins

to make the Emperor's birthday suit!

What a busy week!

The tailors worked without a break.

They spun the thread.

They wove the cloth.

They cut out the pieces.

They sewed them together.

Soon everyone in the palace
was talking about
the Emperor's birthday suit.
A suit that fools couldn't see—
one that was extra special!

On the day before his birthday

the Emperor sent his helpers

to the royal sewing room.

Was the birthday suit ready?

Yes, it was.

Mr. Bobbin held up the jacket.

Mr. Thread held up the pants.

"What do you think?"

asked the tailors.

"It's remarkable!" said one helper.

"I've never seen anything like it!"

said another.

All the other helpers nodded.
None of them wanted
to be called a fool.

The helpers told the Emperor

about his birthday suit.

"Wait till you see it!" they said.

"Words can't describe it!"

The Emperor was tickled.

"We shall have a parade!"
he announced.
"I will wear my royal
birthday suit for all to see...
except, of course, the <u>fools!</u>"
he said.
Everyone laughed.

The next day
the tailors brought the suit
to the Emperor.
"See how the gold threads
shine!" said Mr. Bobbin.
"Ooh!" cried the helpers.
"And see how the silver threads
sparkle," said Mr. Thread.
"Aah!" cried the helpers.

But the Emperor said nothing.

Was he a fool?

His silly helpers were all

oohing and aahing.

Why couldn't he—

the Emperor himself—

see a thing?

"Let us help you put it on,"
said the tailors.

First the pants.

Then the jacket.

The royal helpers crowded around.

"It fits you perfectly!" said one.

"It's definitely <u>you</u>!" said another.

The Emperor grinned.

"Let the parade begin!"

By now the streets
were crowded with people.
Everyone wanted to see
the Emperor's birthday suit—
a suit that only wise people could see!
What would it look like?
First came the horses and riders.
Then came the clowns
and jugglers.

At last the big moment arrived.

A trumpet blared,

and the Emperor came

around the corner.

"Isn't it grand!" cried someone.

"Isn't it amazing!" cried another.

Everyone was oohing and aahing.

Everyone wanted to sound

as wise as the next person.

Suddenly a small voice called out.

"Look, he's not wearing any clothes!"

The band stopped playing.

The horses stopped prancing.

The jugglers stopped juggling.

The flags stopped waving.

"Yes," the crowd whispered.

"The little girl is right!"

The Emperor's face turned bright red.

He was so embarrassed.

Then someone gave him

an old coat.

Another person gave him

an old pair of pants.

The crowd cheered as the Emperor
put on the old clothes.
The Emperor smiled.
Then he began to laugh.

"We were <u>all</u> fools!"

said the Emperor.

"Except this wise little girl.

She was the only one

who was not afraid

to tell the truth.

So I am making her

my head helper!"

Then he lifted her
onto his shoulders
and invited everyone
to the courtyard
for cake and ice cream.

Outside the palace

everyone was laughing.

But inside the palace

Mr. Bobbin and Mr. Thread

were miserable.

The royal guards

had caught them red-handed.

They had been trying to get away

with the six bags of coins!

The Emperor turned

to his new head helper.

"How should we punish these two?"

he asked her.

"Make them sew new clothes
for all the people in the land!"
she said.

"Splendid," said the Emperor.
And this time he made sure
the tailors used cloth
that everyone could see!